Joseph Arnould

Verses, collected and reprinted, as A Memento for Friends

SALZWASSER
VERLAG

Joseph Arnould

Verses, collected and reprinted, as A Memento for Friends

Reprint of the original, first published in 1859.

1st Edition 2022 | ISBN: 978-3-37513-200-2

Verlag (Publisher): Salzwasser Verlag GmbH, Zeilweg 44, 60439 Frankfurt, Deutschland
Vertretungsberechtigt (Authorized to represent): E. Roepke, Zeilweg 44, 60439 Frankfurt, Deutschland
Druck (Print): Books on Demand GmbH, In de Tarpen 42, 22848 Norderstedt, Deutschland

VERSES,

COLLECTED AND REPRINTED, AS

A Memento for Friends.

BY

SIR JOSEPH ARNOULD,

PUISNE JUDGE OF THE SUPREME COURT AT BOMBAY.

LONDON:

PRINTED FOR PRIVATE CIRCULATION.

1859.

CONTENTS.

— ✦ —

HOSPICE OF ST. BERNARD.

(A Prize Poem, recited in the Theatre, Oxford, June 10, 1834 ;
the year of the Duke of Wellington's Installation.)

———◆———

'Οδοιπόρῳ διψῶντι πηγαῖον ῥέος.

Æschyli Agam. 874.

FAST fades the day ; the winds have sunk to sleep,
Monastic Bernard ! on thy lonely steep ;
Like halcyons hov'ring o'er their ocean nest,
The golden clouds are gath'ring into rest
O'er the far peaks, where still the sunset flings
A gleam of splendour from his parting wings,
And stars, like faëry visions, dimly bright,
Now melt in air, now tremble into light.

Night deepens round—the Spirit of Repose
Breathes o'er the darkling crags, and boundless snows :

B

No voice disturbs their gloom ; no living form
Cheers the still scene, or haunts the realms of storm ;
No more the eagle, wheeling to the sky,
Pours through the sullen waste her echoing cry :
The wolf's long howl, that rose upon the gale,
The cataract's roar, the pine-wood's fitful wail,
As the faint chime of some aërial lay   .
Melts from the dreamer's ear, have died away.

    Yes—stern the scene!—magnificently drear !
No sound to ravish, and no sight to cheer ;
Yet to the soul more speaking, than the page
Of loftiest poet, or divinest sage,
Proclaims in characters of heavenly birth,
Graved on the star-lit sky—the slumbering earth,
That He, who framed them both, the Power Divine,
Still in the desert rears his chosen shrine ;
Still loves to commune with his erring child
On the lone mountain, and the pathless wild ;
And, far from human cares, from fev'rish strife,
The storm of passion, and the stir of life ;

When earth breathes peace below, and heav'n above
Is bright with hope, and redolent of love,
He bids each sense awake, each feeling soar,
The spirit kindle, and the heart adore ;
Till to the awe-struck wand'rer's musing breast
E'en Silence speaks, and Solitude is blest.

The stars are forth—the moon serenely bright
Walks in calm beauty through the waste of night ;
Beneath her beams, like silv'ry clouds on high,
The pale snows glimmer in the dark blue sky ;
And as the shadows wander, vale and steep
Now gleam in light, now wrapt in darkness sleep.

Oft at this twilight hour, her quiv'ring rays
Stream through the cliffs, to greet the wanderer's gaze ;
As, faint and worn from many a peril past,
The rushing avalanche, and the roaring blast,
He slowly climbs, where closing mountains lean
In shadowy grandeur, o'er the hush'd ravine ;

Where beneath beetling crags, and drifted snows,
In charnel cell, the unwasting * dead repose ;
And moonlit crosses rising through the gloom,
In spectral silence point the pilgrim's tomb.

   Alike they sleep in that sepulchral grot,
Their death unhonour'd, and their name forgot ;
In life's last hour unsoothed by pitying tear,
Their last deep sigh unheard by mortal ear ;
No coffin guards their clay, no shelt'ring stone,
Their only dirge the wild wind's hollow moan,
When through the grated loopholes, harsh and loud,
Sweeps the chill blast, and waves each eddying shroud—
Well might the wanderer linger there, to scan
The might of Nature and the wreck of Man ;
But lo ! th' ascent is won—the mountain hoar,
The lake's black calm,† the hush'd and frozen shore,

---

* The charnel of the passengers is a small chapel, built under a
cliff to the east of the Hospice, and just within view of it : owing
to the cold, the bodies are long preserved from putrefaction.

† The lake always appears black, from the dazzling whiteness of
the surrounding snows.

And 'mid the snows, yon structure rude and vast,
Rear'd like some rock-built palace of the blast,
Rush on his gaze—and faint, as smiles that play
O'er the wan lips that fade in young decay ;
So cold ! so cheerless !—desolately falls
The misty moonlight on the bleak, gray walls,
Seamed by the scars of Time ; and deeper rents
Stamp'd by the wrath of Men and Elements.
No Sculpture there her gothic tracery weaves,
Piles the tall shaft, or twines the clust'ring leaves ;
But the rude carving of the storm has thrown
A time-worn aspect o'er each mould'ring stone.

Hark ! o'er the lake the choral notes combine,
In mingling cadence, from the lonely shrine ;
The dark-robed brethren of the Hospice there,
Close with a deep-toned hymn their ev'ning prayer ;
While one who long has listen'd to the beat
And far-off echoes of ascending feet,
Still keeps his moonlight watch, and seems to wait
The way-worn wanderer at the welcome gate.

The threshold past—around their frugal board
His toils forgotten, and his strength restored ;
As the red pine-fire throws a flickering blaze
O'er the rude hall, delighted shall he gaze
On many a lofty brow, and speaking eye,
In that unknown, yet friendly company ;—
While the blithe laugh, and pleasure-stirring sound
Of cheerful converse, gaily echoes round,
As from the stranger of the world below,
They learn the changeful tale of weal and woe.

Oh ! other lyres of graver tone may praise
The convent's wakeful nights, and languid days ;
Religion bids me weep—and Reason sigh
O'er the lorn heart's uncheer'd captivity,
That chills each tenderer impulse, and reproves
What Heav'n has sanction'd, and what Nature loves :
By priestly craft, or jealous power design'd
To curb the aspirings of the manly mind ;
While Genius pines, and Feeling's early flowers,
Droop in the sickly shade of joyless hours.

Not mine to laud the penance, and the chain,
Ascetic toils, or self-inflicted pain ;
Or trace to heavenly source the zeal that piled
Fond Simeon's pillar in the Syrian wild ;*
Or that false faith whose meteor-smile illumes
La Trappe's cold cells, or Nubia's peopled tombs ;†
Where dark-brow'd zealots vex the weary nights
With ghastly orgies, and mysterious rites,
Breathe 'mid remorseful sighs the frequent prayer,
Live without love, scarce die without despair.

Such are Devotion's feverish dreams, that ply
The fool with taunts, and wake the wise man's sigh ;
Far loftier hopes St. Bernard's sons allure,
Their faith erroneous, but their practice pure ;
And nobler ardour nerves their hearts to mock
The frost's keen power, and brave the tempest's
  shock.

---

 * Simeon Stylites lived forty-five years in the Syrian desert, on a pillar gradually raised till it reached the height of sixty feet.

 † The ruined tombs of Upper Egypt are (or were) filled by monks of the sternest cast.—GIBBON, vol. vi.

The ling'ring memories of departed hours,
Youth's worshipp'd dreams, and beauty's roseate bowers,
Th' unbidden thoughts that kindle fond regret
For joys e'en virtue cannot all forget,
Come soften'd through the calm : Earth's sorrows wind
A sweet sad influence o'er the musing mind,
Felt, but to vanish, like the hues that glow
In Summer's twilight on the mountain snow.

Theirs is the sunshine of the heart, that springs
From high-soul'd deeds, and heav'n-taught sufferings ;
Theirs the pure love no laws of sect can bind,
Their creed to soothe the sorrows of mankind ;
And theirs the precept—more can angels teach ?—
To live for God, and act the truths they preach ;
And freely fly, unconscious of dismay,
Where Pity prompts, and Courage points the way.

Yes ! oft at night's dread noon, when gales are loud,
And shapes of terror ride the murky cloud ;

When the white snow-waves,* drifting silently,
Wreathe o'er the rocks, and roll along the sky ;—
'Tis theirs, at Mercy's call, to brave the wrath
That guides the avalanche on his thundering path,
Waked by the mastiff's bay :—A faint, low shriek
Is echoing far below, from cave and peak,
By some lone wanderer pour'd, whose latest breath
Is all concenter'd in that cry of death ;
Thrilling, and fearful, as the rushing snows
Sweep on, and shroud him in their dire repose.
" On, fearless on ! and trace him through the storm !
Still in his veins the pulse of life beats warm ;
The dog's deep wailing howl our steps shall guide,
Near and more near it climbs the mountain side."
Swift on their iron poles from steep to steep,
From crag to crag, impetuous down they sweep ;
Like spectres thread the dark ravine—and lo !
The strong dog crouching o'er the tomb of snow
Plies with untiring limb his generous toil,
Scoops the cold drift, and bares the frozen soil ;

* Rogers' " Italy."

Licks from the pale chill brow the tangled hair,
And wakes to Hope the features of Despair ;
Till from the cerements of his living tomb
They raise the wanderer, while the paly bloom
Of coming life plays warmly on his cheek,
And those half-op'ning lips do all but speak.

Deeds such as these, while quickly wears the night,
In that rude hall St. Bernard's sons recite—
And oft they speak of crags, where peasants show
Mysterious crosses on the untrodden snow *
Planted by hands unseen, or traces left
Of wizard dances in the sunless cleft ;
Or whisp'ring tell, when clouds snow-laden sail
At solemn midnight on the moaning gale,
How on each cavern'd steep, in shadowy forms,
The demon-brood of Darkness and of Storms
Shout in wild chorus, while on every blast
Weird voices sweep, and laughter hurries past :

* Vide Wordsworth's " Descriptive Sketches.''

Oft too in gentler shape, they seem to ride
In mimic pomp, the mists of eventide ;
Or move unmark'd within their vapoury shroud,
The winds their coursers, and their car the cloud ;
While from their stringless lyres wild music flows,
Charms the mute air, and dies along the snows.*

Such the fond faith in every age confest,
Nursed by each clime, and rear'd in every breast,
The secret yearning, the mysterious sense
Of some unseen, o'ershadowing influence,
That taught the Greek to people earth and sky
With forms of light and dreams of poesy ;
Which teaches still the savage and the child,
Their heart untutor'd, and their fancy wild,
To vision spirits of the viewless breeze,
Phantoms in clouds, and voices on the seas ;
And on th' expanse of Heav'n's eternal dome
Fix their fond gaze, and weep that long lost home.

* For these and other superstitions of the Alpine peasantry, see
Coxe's " Tour," and Wordsworth's " Descriptive Sketches."

But when the lamp burns faintly, and the guest
Seeks his low cell, and homely couch of rest,
Dim with the mists of time before his eyes
Majestic forms of other days arise,
And to his ear the night-winds waft along
Names that have lived in story or in song.

Once more the foe of Rome from height to height *
Cheers his dark host, impatient for the fight,
And where yon plains expand in boundless gloom,
He bids them seek an Empire or a Tomb.
With nodding plumes, bright helms, and glitt'ring spears,
Lo Gaul's great Emperor leads his knightly peers ; *
Hush'd is their iron tramp, and moonbeams dim
Show'r on each ghastly brow and mail-clad limb.
He too is there, who, slain on victory's day,
Beside their altar sleeps, the young Dessaix ; †

---

* Both Hannibal and Charlemagne, in all probability, took quite
a different route. But a tradition still remains of their having
passed by the Great St. Bernard.

† Dessaix, slain in his thirtieth year at the battle of Marengo, to

And there his Chief, whose name of terror spread

Wide o'er the world, and shook mankind with dread,

Curbs his proud steed, and waves his warriors on

To Piedmont's vales yet "bright with Lodi's
     sun ; " *

Unlike the despot lord of after days,

Youth on his cheek, and ardour in his gaze ;

E'en now his spirit from the fields of fight

The shout of triumph hears, the rush of flight,

As from Marengo's plain, " th' invading horde "†

Flies the keen vengeance of his conqu'ring sword.

Changed is his brow, what loftier visions roll,

What dreams of empire crowd upon his soul !

Lo ! prostrate nations tremble at his sway,

Kings quail before him, thrones in dust decay ;

Dominion crowns what Conquest has begun,

And Fortune, smiling on her favourite son,

the success of which he had chiefly contributed, is buried near the
altar of the Hospice Church.

   * A phrase of Buonaparte, in addressing Bourienne before passing
the Alps to Marengo.—BOURIENNE, vol. ii.

   † Napoleon's invariable term for the Austrians in Italy.—BOU-
RIENNE, *passim.*

Wreathes round his tyrant brow the glitt'ring toy,
Her fatal dower, that shines but to destroy.

If in that hour of pride, and fervid youth,
Such were his dreams, mankind has mourn'd their truth ;
O'er seas of blood his Sun of Glory rose,
And sunk at length 'mid tempest to repose.
When on that field, where last the eagle soar'd ;
War's mightier master wielded Britain's sword,
And the dark soul, a world could scarce subdue,
Bent to thy genius—CHIEF of WATERLOO !

The visions fade in darkness, calm and deep
Sinks o'er the pilgrim's soul the hush of sleep.
Farewell ! farewell ! ere morning's sun shall smile,
Desolate mansion ! on thy wind-worn pile,
Far to the South his parting steps shall bend,
Where lovelier lands, and softer skies extend ;
Yet in those climes full oft his heart shall seek
Those sable waters, and that frozen peak ;

'Mid fairer scenes shall rise on Fancy's view
Th' eternal snows, the heaven of cloudless blue ;
And as in thought once more he seems to climb
O'er many a trackless Alp, and cliff sublime,
Kind priests of Charity ! ye oft shall share
The heartfelt breathings of his grateful prayer ;
While Memory turns to bless, where'er he roam,
Love's sainted shrine, and Mercy's lonely home !

LORD DENMAN.

———

At a Meeting of the Home Circuit Mess, held at Kingston-on-Thames, on the 2nd of April, 1850, at which the accompanying verses were recited by the Poet Laureate, it was unanimously resolved that the verses should be printed, and a copy sent to each member of the circuit; and also that a manuscript copy, both of the verses and of the resolution, should be forwarded to Lord Denman.

———

Forgive your Laureate if he flings away
His motley mask, and dares be grave to-day,
While to the memory of a great career
He yields a homage, feeble—but sincere.

A noble race is ended;—from the noise
Of Life's arena to the tranquil joys
Of wise seclusion, glorious with a crown
Of civic worth and dignified renown

DENMAN retires ; and leaves a lofty name
To the sure keeping of historic fame.
Long shall the name of DENMAN live enshrined
In the fond reverence of the English mind ;
Rich as he was in every manly grace
That stamps the sons of England's hero race ;
True Saxon worth cast in the stately mould
Of the old Roman ; stern and lion-soul'd ;
Yet touch'd by kindlier impulses that move
The hearts, that else had but admired, to love.

England remembers how in manhood's flower,
The bold assailant of all lawless power,
His voice was lifted loudest in the van
Of those who fought against the trade in man :
England has not forgotten how the rush
Of his fierce eloquence roll'd forth to crush
The courtly crew who, to appease the spleen
Of a King's spite, would immolate a Queen :
Nor how, with front erect, he trod the path
Of Justice, heedless of a Senate's wrath ;

And, firm for rights our Fathers handed down,
Withstood the House, as he had braved the Crown.

Throned on the seat of judgment, he combined
The purest purpose with the widest mind :
His aim was always Justice ; his delight
To render Law commensurate with Right,
And from the breadth of that august domain
Weed the rank growth of quibbling and chicane :
No zealot votary of the cumbrous lore
That " darken'd counsel " in the days of yore ;
Not blindly worshipping as things divine
The dust and cobwebs of the legal shrine ;
But bent to make,—so taught in Wisdom's school,—
Our laws progressive, like the realm they rule.

His proud demeanour and majestic grace
Suited the height of his illustrious place :
Blended extremes in him we could admire,
MURRAY's fine ease, and CHATHAM's generous fire ;

Calmly sedate and equably polite
He felt no preference, and he show'd no slight ;
Not prone to talk, but diligent to hear ;
Prompt, and yet patient ; firm, but not austere ;
Not quick to wrath, but when fit cause arose
To stir his lion-nature from repose,—
Some deed of baseness, cruelty, or shame—
Swift shot the electric impulse thro' his frame ;
The grave brow lower'd ; the eye so calm and cold
Flash'd sudden fire ; and forth in thunder roll'd
The voice whose accents clothed with solemn awe
The indignant doom of violated law.

DENMAN farewell ! forgive the attempt to twine
A wreath so worthless for a brow like thine :
But while all others hasten to salute
Thy name with honour, how can *we* be mute ?
We who have known thee long, and watch'd thee near
Dispensing Justice in our narrower sphere ;
Who feel thy loss not more to be deplored
On the grave bench than at the genial board,—

That festive scene where thou didst love to sit,
Promoting manly mirth and honest wit,
Where not a guest, howe'er "unknown to fame,"
But heard thy deep voice pledge him by his name,
While proudly through our hearts the feeling ran—
" *All must revere the Judge, we love the Man.*"

   Once more farewell ! may every blessing wait
On thy retirement, to a distant date !
May all the pleasures of a taste refined,
And all the affluence of a well-stored mind,
And all the affections of a loving breast,
Solace thy age, and sanctify thy rest.

SIR ROBERT PEEL.

—◆—

Αἴλινον, αἴλινον εἰπὲ, τὸ δ' εὖ νικάτω.

DEAD : housed with dust and darkness !—he who sate
But yesterday in more than monarch's state,
Throned in the heart of England with a crown
Of self-earn'd kingship—suddenly struck down
From the mid heaven of greatness—how it all
Seems like a dream—that glory and that fall !

With dim despondence and a bodeful gloom
England sits sad by that untimely tomb ;
Her chief of statesmen gone, his work remains
For hands less skilful and for feebler brains :—
The keen, swift insight,—the capacious soul
That analysed all parts, yet grasp'd the whole,—

The fix'd laboriousness that calmly wrought
Truth from the mines of scientific thought,—
The master skill which, when that truth was won,
Made other minds the mirror of his own,
And bound with spells of intellectual might
The sons of darkness in their own despite,—
The manly march of vigorous eloquence,
The sober style of poised and weighty sense
Clear to convince and potent to persuade,
Wrought with high art, yet free from art's parade,—
The dexterous logic, the high-toned appeal,
The skill to move men's mirth, or rouse their zeal,—
All the rare powers which, when combined, create
Their envied lord the despot of debate,—
All these were his—but not alone for these
A nation's homage crowns his obsequies ;
What England mourns is something nobler far
Than mightiest mastery in the mimic war,
Wisdom achieved by virtue—wisdom earn'd
By trampling on the idols he had learn'd
To venerate amiss—the inbred love
Of Truth and Country lifting him above

The fond traditions, and the servile rules
That nursed his youth amid those famous schools
Where mists of prejudice with noxious damp
Dim the pale beam of learning's classic lamp.—
Long was the struggle—long the cloister's chill
Deaden'd his spirit and subdued his will ;
But Truth upheld her votary ; and the light
Clearer and clearer stream'd upon his sight,
As with strong effort struggling to unwind
The snaky coils of Error from his mind,
He smote the foul enchantress—till at length
Fell the last fold that manacled his strength,
And left his unthrall'd manhood free to dare
Deeds which all else had shrunk from in despair.

Twice upon England's annals hath he set
A mark no after ages shall forget.
Once when he swept away the bigot laws
That outraged Freedom in Religion's cause,
That from men's rituals made their rights proceed,
And risk'd a Realm to persecute a Creed :

And once when bending to the mighty cry

By hungering myriads lifted to the sky,

He spoke the word and gave the great decree,

" Let Bread be tax'd no more—and Trade be free !"

Glory to him who resolutely great

Twice wreck'd his Party and twice saved the State ;

Whose well-timed daring kept Victoria's crown

Firm in the storm when Europe's thrones went
      down.

What though for this high stake he flung away

The prize of power, and all the pomp of sway—

A people's blessing well might compensate

The rhetorician's sneer, the zealot's hate,

And England's homage nobly made amends

For faithless followers and for failing friends.

Yes ! by those hearths that he has help'd to cheer,

His memory shall abide for many a year ;

And the swart sons of toil as they recruit

Their task-worn strength with Earth's abundant
      fruit

No longer leaven'd by the sense of wrong,
Shall breathe his name with blessings loud and
    long.*

That name is mourn'd upon the crowded mart,
And mourn'd no less thro' all the realms of Art—
Genius and Industry their voices blend
In mutual dirges for their noblest friend.
And there are deeper mourners for the Dead—
But o'er their grief be sacred silence spread ;
One voice, now dumb with woe, alone could tell
How good, how pure the heart she loved so well.

Mother of mighty sons, my Country—thou
That sit'st in sorrow—clear thy clouded brow.

---

* " It may be that I shall leave a name sometimes remembered
with good will in the abode of those whose lot it is to labour and to
earn their daily bread by the sweat of their brow, when they shall
recruit their exhausted strength with abundant and untaxed food,
the sweeter because it is no longer leavened with a sense of
injustice."

A good great man nor lives nor dies in vain ;
A beacon star o'er Life's tumultuous main
Shines from his grave of glory : many tread `
In pathways hallow'd by the mighty dead.
Statesmen unborn from him shall learn the way
That leads thro' manful worth to solid sway,
And strive to scale Ambition's steepy hill
By virtuous wisdom, not by tortuous skill.
Can he who gazes on that honour'd grave
Stoop to be Faction's tool or Party's slave ?—
Or who can trace the lines to glory dear,
By generous France inscribed upon that bier—
Or catch the echoes, as the mournful tale
Wide o'er the nations wakes the voice of wail,—
Nor burn to kindle such a loving zeal
As thrills through Europe for the fame of PEEL !

July, 1850.

HAVELOCK.

He sleeps the sleep of heroes ; and for him
Stern hearts are sad, and manly eyes are dim :
What though the tardy title that they gave
To grace the warrior, found him in his grave ;
The loss is ours—not his ; our Havelock needs
No vulgar blazon for his deathless deeds.

No plaudits loud, no faint-praise trimly turn'd
Could make or mar the glory he had earn'd :
The love of England is a nobler prize
Than Senates can decree or Kings devise ;
And England's grief a statelier monument
Than wealth can build, or heraldry invent.

Yes, England loved this warrior, for she felt
That in his soul true English virtue dwelt.

Steadfast, yet ardent, prompt but wary, brave
To height of daring, yet not daring's slave ;
Pious as valiant, hopeful 'mid despair ;
Calm under fire, but passionate in prayer :
Alike in peace and war, one path he trod,
His law was Duty, and his guide was GOD.

Through arduous struggles and with toil severe,
His friendless virtue plough'd its slow career,
He could not match in purse the carpet lords
Of purchased epaulettes, and bauble swords ;
Merit, not wealth, when manhood's prime was past,
Raised the born leader to command at last :
And with command came glory.   Why recall
What lives and burns within the hearts of all ?
We all remember how he rose—a star—
On the thick midnight of that dreadful war,
Roll'd back the tide of ruin, and restored
The poise of Empire with his single sword.

We all remember how through India's plains,
Scorch'd by fierce suns, or drench'd by tropic rains,

O'er steamy swamps by torrid skies o'er-arch'd,

Dauntless and swift, the heroic handful march'd.

No need to count their triumphs, none to tell

Of cursed Cawnpore, and its hideous well ;

Of Lucknow's fate, that trembled on a thread,

Of the fierce carnage, and the glorious dead ;

When the close battery's tempest surged and sung,

And through a lane of fire the avengers sprung,

Spent, but victorious—and the glorious shout

For Lucknow's rescue scared the miscreant rout—

Yes, they were saved, but at what deadly cost !

The ransom'd live ; but what a ransom 's lost !

His brain outwearied and his heart o'erfraught,

The avenger sinks beside the work he wrought.

He lived to save ; and, having saved, bow'd down

Beneath the burden of his great renown;

Leaving to us the treasure of his fame,

A noble memory and a stainless name.

DAILY NEWS, *Jan.* 12, 1858.

EPITHALAMIUM.

—◆—

All hearts and hopes are with thee at this hour,
Thou fair young bride ! of English brides the flower ;
Thou of the frank high-heart, and Saxon mien,
The first-born daughter of our best-loved Queen.
All in thy joy are joyful, for we know
This royal pomp is no mere gilded show,
No cold state-pageant, but a rite that binds
With holy ties " a marriage of true minds."
The willing work of thy white hand creates
A bond of union for two mighty States :
But more than this—its genial clasp imparts
A glow of rapture to two loving hearts.

Swift speed the years; but yesterday the voice
Of those hoarse heralds bade the realm rejoice
At thy auspicious dawning into life,
And now their thunders welcome thee—a wife.

Brief was thy virgin youth—but not too short
To learn those lessons rarely conn'd at Court—
The piety, whose roots are hearts, not creeds,
Whose fruits are gentle lives and noble deeds ;
The wisdom never taught by text or tome ;
The living sermon of a virtuous home.

Thy mother is thy model ; be like her :
No choicer boon thy Queenship can confer
On thy lord's future lieges : the firm mind,
The truthful nature, simple yet refined,
The high clear courage, and the noble zeal
For England's glory and the Empire's weal,
The pure affections, and the spotless life
Of the fond mother and the loving wife ;—
Graces like these have made Victoria great,
And kept her safe 'mid all the storms of state,
Founding her throne on that unshaken base—
The loving homage of a free-born race.

Thou, too, young Prince ! by holiest bonds allied
To the proud realm that rear'd thy island bride,

Learn here the lore contented millions teach—
Free trade, free thought, free worship, and free speech.
Deep in thy heart the generous seed be sown,
And let it bear rich fruitage round thy throne ;
Rule as they rule in England—let no trace
Of feudal folly vex that loyal race
Which, ripe for freedom, struggles to be free,
And, tired of pedants, hopes plain sense from thee.

Farewell ! be great and happy—may the years
Be liberal of smiles and scant in tears.
May children bless your life, and build your line :
With homefelt bliss a people's love combine ;
So may ye reign—no words can wish you more—
As Albert and Victoria reign'd before.

DAILY NEWS, *Jan.* 25, 1858.